SEBASTIAN
The tale of a curious kitten

Vanessa Julian-Ottie

This is Sebastian, always the odd
one out, heading for the cat door.
"Where are you off to, Sebastian?
Come back!" called Mother Cat.

Sebastian paid no attention.
He was already outside,
sniffing new smells and
hearing new sounds.

"What's that? Who's there?"
Sebastian gathered up his paws
and jumped through the hole
in the rocks.

"Ow! Ow! Ow!" cried Sebastian.
"Porcupines hurt!"

Sebastian limped towards the fence.
He was annoyed.
"Just a minute," he said, "what kind
of animal is that?"

"Hello," said the goat.
"Hello, hello," said the ducks.
"Where are you going?"
But Sebastian limped by and never
said a word. He felt silly.

Beyond the duck pond was a drainpipe.
Sebastian looked and looked.
Was that a mouse at the other end?
He pounced.

Kersplash!
Where did that mouse go?